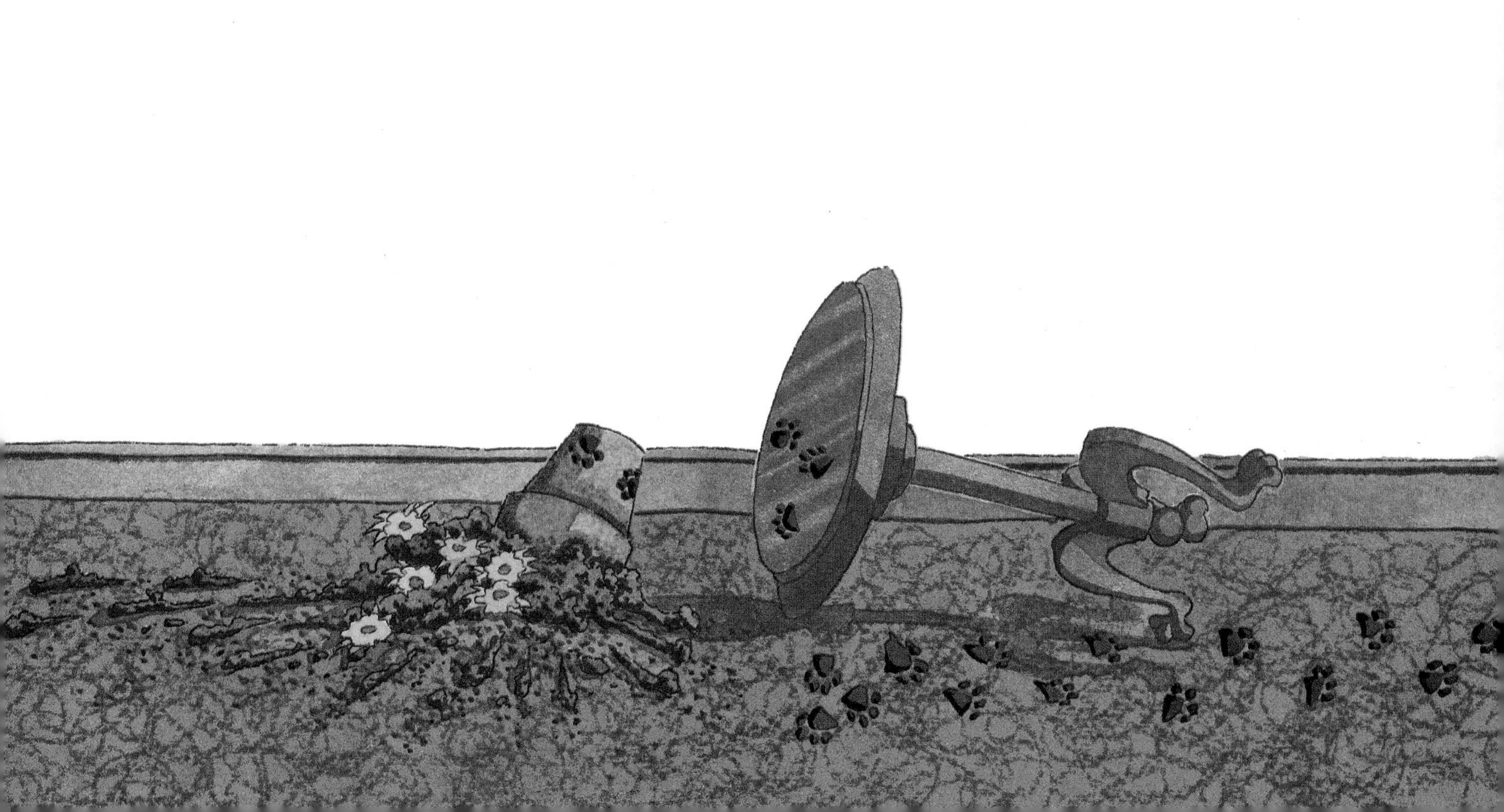

ISBN-13: 978-0-439-89542-2
ISBN-10: 0-439-89542-1

Text and illustrations copyright © 2005 by Nick Bruel. All rights reserved. Published by Scholastic Inc., 557 Broadway, New York, NY 10012, by arrangement with Roaring Brook Press, a division of Holtzbrinck Publishing Holdings Limited Partnership.

FOR CARINA

12 11 10 9 8 7 6 5 4
7 8 9 10 11/0

Printed in the U.S.A.   40

First Scholastic printing, November 2006

She
wasn't
always
a
bad
kitty.

She used to be a good kitty,

until one day . . .

OH, DEAR! WE'RE ALL OUT OF FOOD FOR THE KITTY!

ALL WE HAVE ARE SOME HEALTHY AND DELICIOUS...

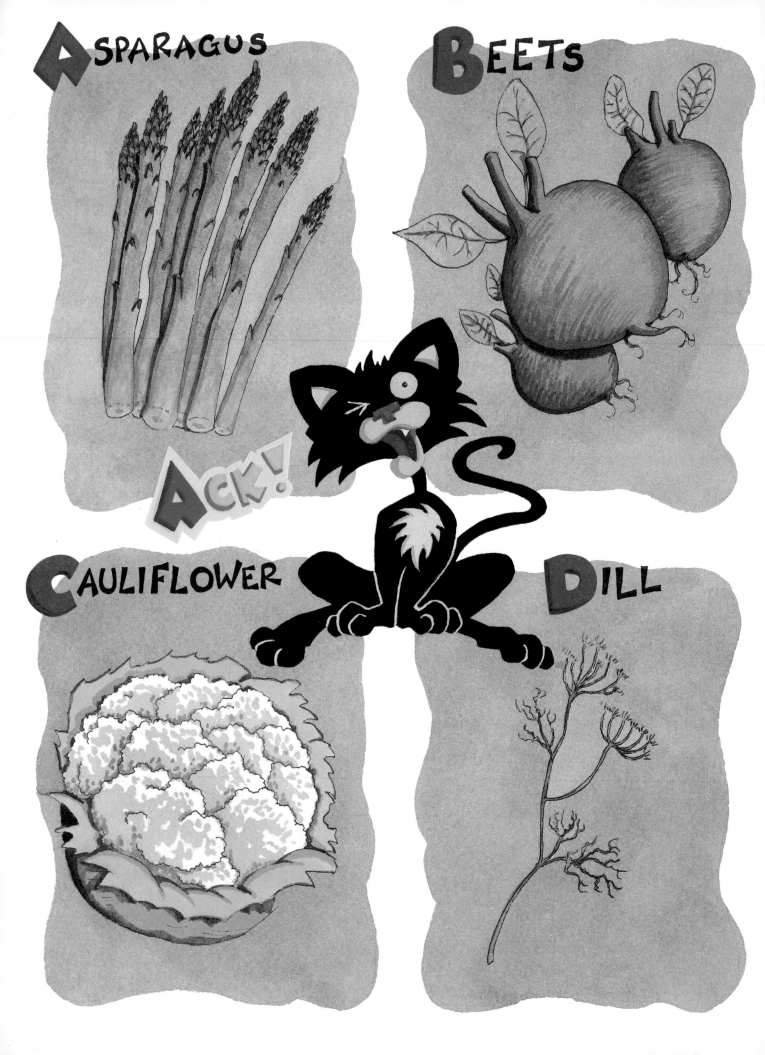

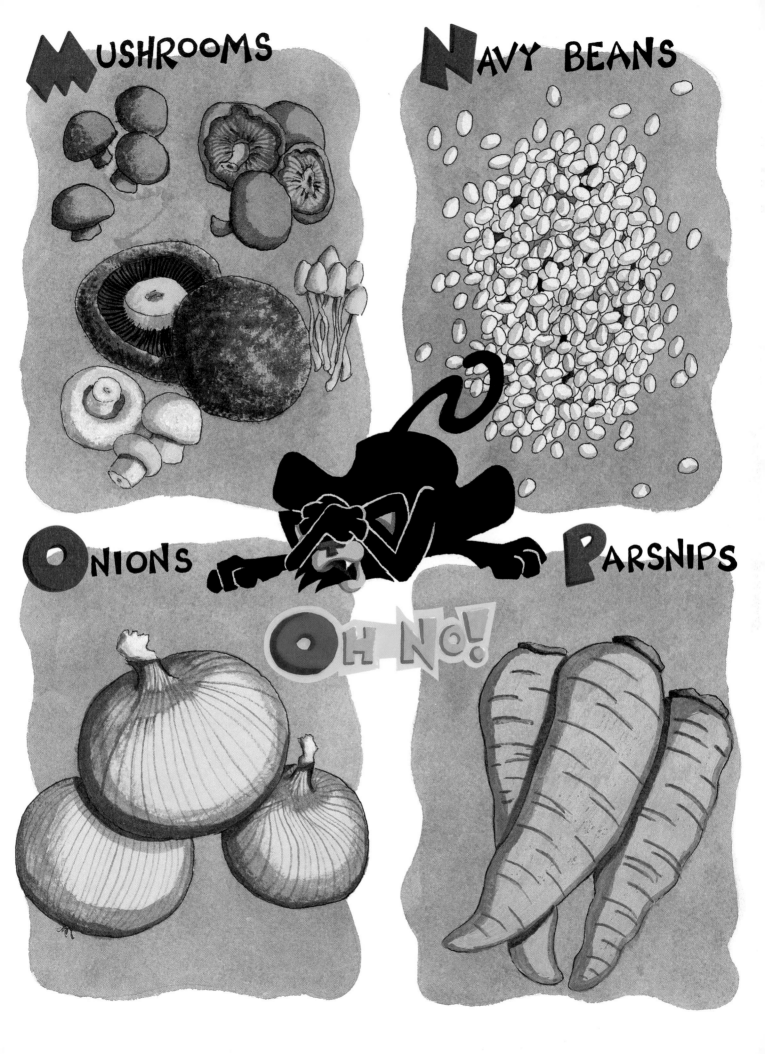

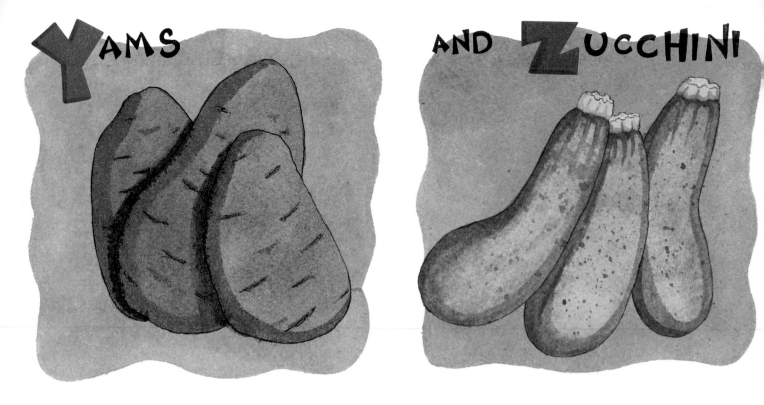

YAMS AND **Z**UCCHINI

Kitty was not happy.
Not happy at all.

That's when she decided
she would be a
BAD kitty.

But not just any bad
kitty—a very, very, bad,
bad, BAD kitty.

She . . .

WAS **M**EAN TO MY MOMMY

WAS **N**ASTY TO DADDY'S NECKTIES

OVERTURNED HER CAT BOX

PLOTTED AGAINST US

What a bad kitty.

What a very, very, bad, bad, bad kitty.

But then . . .

I'M BACK FROM THE GROCERY STORE! LOOK AT ALL THE GOOD FOOD I BOUGHT FOR KITTY!

WE HAVE...

Yak Yogurt **and Baked Zebra Ziti**

Now, kitty was happy!
Very, very happy!

She decided that from
now on, she would be
a GOOD kitty!

But not just any good
kitty—a very, very,
good, good, good,
kitty!

She . . .

QUIT QUARRELING WITH OUR NEIGHBOR

DEAR NEIGHBOR,
PURR PURRR
PURR PURR
PURRR PURR
PURR!
SINCERELY,

REPAIRED THE CURTAINS

SAVED THE DAY

TIED MY SHOES

What a good kitty!
What a very, very good, good, good kitty!

How can we reward such a good kitty?

I know . . .

Uh-oh . . .